D0462246

Scholastic Canada Ltd.

604 King Street West, Toronto, Ontario M5V 1E1, Canada

Scholastic Inc.

557 Broadway, New York, NY 10012, USA

Scholastic Australia Pty Limited

PO Box 579, Gosford, NSW 2250, Australia

Scholastic New Zealand Limited

Private Bag 94407, Botany, Manukau 2163, New Zealand

Scholastic Children's Books

Euston House, 24 Eversholt Street, London NW1 1DB, UK

Library and Archives Canada Cataloguing in Publication

Larry, H. I.

Deep waters / H.I. Larry ; Ash Oswald, illustrator.

(Zac Power)

ISBN 978-0-545-99915-1

I. Oswald, Ash II. Title. III. Series : Larry, H. I. Zac Power.

PZ7.L333De 2007   j823   C2007-903774-7

ISBN 10: 0-545-99915-4

Illustration and design by Ash Oswald

With special thanks to the spies of

years 2 and 3 (2005) of the St Michael's unit of GIB

for their top-secret mission support.

6 5 4 3 2   Printed in Canada 121   12 13 14 15 16

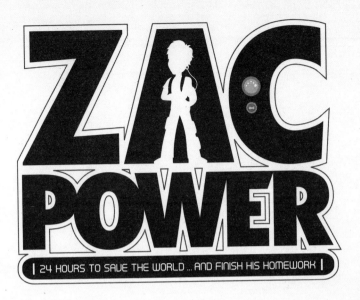

ZAC POWER

| 24 HOURS TO SAVE THE WORLD ... AND FINISH HIS HOMEWORK |

DEEP WATERS

BY *H. I. LARRY*

ILLUSTRATIONS BY *ASH OSWALD*

Scholastic Canada Ltd.
Toronto New York London Auckland Sydney
Mexico City New Delhi Hong Kong Buenos Aires

CHAPTER...ONE

Zac couldn't help it. He was trying to look interested in what the tour guide at the West Sea Aquarium was saying, but could he help it if his eyes kept closing all by themselves?

"Zac Power!" hissed his teacher, Mrs. Tran. "I suggest you pay attention. There'll be a test after the excursion, you know."

Zac's eyes snapped open.

"Coral might not look exciting…" the tour guide was saying.

He's right there, thought Zac, checking his watch yet again. How could it still only be 9:03 a.m.?

"…but did you know coral takes over a million years to form?"

A million years!

Surely he wouldn't be stuck at the aquarium that long!

Zac stared out the window. The aquarium was on the edge of the West Sea. Zac saw perfect surfing waves breaking.

If only he was out there instead of being stuck in here…

"I'll pass around some coral," said the tour guide. "Can you feel how rough it is?"

Zac stood with his arms crossed. He'd had more fun sorting his sock drawer!

"Let's move on to our next exhibit, kids," the tour guide went on. "The shark tank!"

Zac woke right up. *Sharks! Maybe there'll be great white sharks with huge, bloody teeth!*

"Onto the moving walkway," called the tour guide.

The moving walkway was a flat escalator snaking all around the aquarium. The whole class stepped on and moved slowly toward the shark tank.

"It's feeding time," said the tour guide, sounding excited.

Zac craned his neck to see. Inside the tank were two divers with hunks of meat in their hands. Four sharks were swimming straight for them. The sharks were massive!

"Don't worry, everybody," said the tour guide. "The sharks really want that meat. It only *looks* like they're attacking the divers!"

The sharks circled around the divers. The water churned.

"Wait – they really *are* attacking the divers!" shrieked the tour guide.

A shark had one of the divers by the leg.

"Shark attack!" Mrs. Tran yelled.

Suddenly, everyone in the aquarium was screaming. People were running right and left. The tour guide hid under a chair.

In all the confusion, Zac felt a tap on his shoulder.

"Zac Power?" a voice said.

Zac turned around. Beside him stood a giant turtle. Or, to be exact, a woman dressed in a turtle costume.

"Come and look at the baby turtle exhibit," said the giant turtle woman.

Baby turtles? What was this woman talking about? There was a shark attack on!

Zac wanted to help.

Or, at the very least, watch.

"Ah, no thanks. I'll stay here," Zac said firmly.

"No, come with me. Now!"

Suddenly, the walkway started moving under Zac's feet. But this time it wasn't going slowly. It was speeding Zac and the giant turtle woman toward the baby turtle exhibit. Next door, Zac could still hear screaming.

"It's not a real shark attack," explained the giant turtle. "GIB hired stunt divers to create a diversion while we sent you on your next mission."

GIB, or Government Investigation Bureau, was the spy agency Zac worked for. The woman pushed up the bright green sleeves of her turtle costume. Zac saw a miniature walkie-talkie strapped to her wrist. She tapped it once and then spoke into it.

"Attention all GIB ground staff. This is Big Turtle. Do you read me?"

The walkie-talkie crackled.

"Loud and clear, Big Turtle," came the reply. "The amphibious submersible is good to go."

The water in the turtle exhibit started bubbling. Then, the coolest thing Zac had ever seen rose up from behind a clump of seaweed. The top was glass. There were wings on the sides and rockets on the

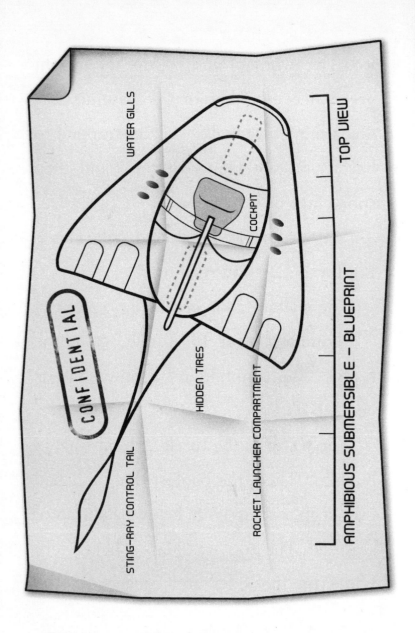

CONFIDENTIAL

WATER GILLS

COCKPIT

STING-RAY CONTROL TAIL

HIDDEN TIRES

ROCKET LAUNCHER COMPARTMENT

TOP VIEW

AMPHIBIOUS SUBMERSIBLE – BLUEPRINT

back. Underneath were two fat tires.

"What is it?" said Zac, who couldn't help being impressed.

"An amphibious submersible. It goes under water like a submarine and across land too."

Big Turtle handed Zac a set of keys.

"Ever piloted one before?" she asked.

Zac shook his head.

He didn't know what his next mission was, but he didn't care. Wherever he was going, he was going there in the amphibious submersible.

It sure beat learning about coral!

CHAPTER...
...TWO

Right, thought Zac to himself, as he settled back in the amphibious submersible's cockpit, *how hard can it really be to pilot this thing?*

Zac's brother Leon would have known exactly how to get the amphibious submersible started. The entire Power family were spies, but Leon was the techno-geek of the family. But after Zac almost single-handedly completed their Poison Island mission and saved Leon's life, GIB had decided Zac was ready for his first solo mission.

Leon was transferred from Field Agent to Technical Officer. It seemed like the perfect arrangement to both of them.

Zac looked at the panel of dials and flashing lights in front of him. There was no simple "on" button, or anywhere obvious to put the ignition key.

The briefest doubt flickered through his mind. If he couldn't even figure out how to pilot an amphibious submersible, was he really ready for a solo mission? But when it came to his talents, Zac never wasted much time doubting himself. *Of course* he was ready to be a solo spy – even if he was still only 12 years old.

Zac fished around in the seat pocket for the instruction manual. There it was – and it was about as thick as his math textbook!

There was no way Zac was reading all that boring stuff. He flicked straight to the last page and quickly scanned it. Then he chucked the whole thing over his shoulder and into the trash.

He pressed a green button, and then a flashing yellow one. The amphibious submersible's engine responded with a series of very loud, very satisfying revs.

Then a dial labelled "speed control" caught Zac's eye. He turned it up as far as it would go. The amphibious submersible shot forward!

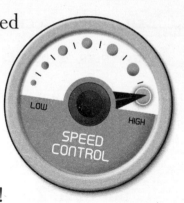

A thrill raced through Zac's body. *This was way better than a school excursion, staring into boring old fish tanks.*

Fish tanks?

Suddenly, Zac remembered he was still inside the turtle tank at the aquarium. The amphibious submersible was racing at top speed toward a huge glass wall that stood between him and the West Sea.

Frantically, Zac looked around for the

exit. There seemed to be no way out. *Was there a button on the dashboard that would somehow slide the glass aside?* Zac wondered. *It was probably somewhere in the instruction manual.*

But then, Zac hadn't read it!

Faster and faster Zac sped toward the glass wall. If he hit it, the glass would break into a million pieces. And Zac didn't like to think what would happen to the amphibious submersible!

Then Zac saw something. The glove compartment! He popped it open. Inside, he saw a remote control that looked exactly like his garage-door opener at home. He hit the big red button on the top.

The glass wall began to slide out of the way! Zac shot through the gap with only millimetres to spare. He was out in the open sea.

Zac pulled down the visor in front of him to check his hair. And there, taped right across the mirror was a small metal disc with a note attached.

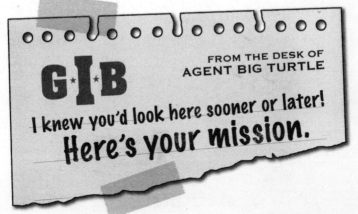

FROM THE DESK OF
AGENT BIG TURTLE

GIB

I knew you'd look here sooner or later!
Here's your mission.

Zac sighed. The fun was over. It was time for work again.

He pulled his SpyPad from his pocket. A SpyPad looks a bit like an electronic game but it is actually a mini-computer, satellite mobile phone and laser, all rolled into one. Every GIB spy has to have one.

Zac loaded the disc into his SpyPad.

■■■■■■■■

CLASSIFIED
FOR THE EYES OF ZAC POWER ONLY

MISSION RECEIVED
TUESDAY 9:45AM

Top-secret sources tell us a new type
of submarine has been invented.

An ordinary submarine can
dive 450 metres below sea level.
Rumour has it this new sub can
dive 1,200 metres below sea level.

The new submarine is due to be tested
somewhere in the West Sea
in the next 24 hours.

YOUR MISSION

• Locate secret submarine.
• Discover who is behind it
and what they plan to do with it.

END

   WATERPROOF MODE
>>> ON

He'd gotten out of school, was piloting the coolest amphibious submersible ever and all he had to do was find some submarine? So far this mission was working out well!

CHAPTER... ...THREE

One thing was for sure, thought Zac. *The secret submarine would need to be tested in water at least 1,200 metres deep.* And that could only be a long way away from shore.

Zac was going to have to set a course right out to the middle of the ocean. And if that meant he could squeeze in a little joyride on the way...well, that was *almost* part of the job.

Flicking the autopilot switch, Zac stuck his feet up on the dashboard. He plugged in his iPod and speakers and turned the music up really loud. His satellite GPS navigation software could handle the directions. It was made by Marine Tech. Zac knew this small company somehow always came out with the coolest sea technology just before the bigger companies did.

Zac typed in the coordinates for the middle of the sea, where the water was deepest. At least, he *thought* he did.

He must have hit the wrong button, because the next second the amphibious submersible was upside down and spinning round and round in circles.

The foghorn was blaring, the cabin lights were flashing on and off and the fire sprinklers activated.

Just then, Zac heard his SpyPad beeping.

He picked it up.

It was Leon calling! This was going to be embarrassing.

CALLER
>>>
LEON POWER
-AGENT TECHNO GEEK-

ACCEPT
>>> YES

SHARK ALARM
>>> ON

"Zac here," he said, trying to sound like he had things totally under control.

"What's all that noise, Zac?" asked Leon anxiously. "Are you OK?"

"I'm fine," Zac snapped, holding a bucket under the fire sprinkler and trying to muffle the foghorn with a towel.

"*Sure* you understand how to operate the submersible?" asked Leon.

"Of course!" said Zac, breezily. The submersible spun round and round. He was going to be sick any second.

"OK," said Leon doubtfully. "Listen, I've got new information about the mission from our mole at Marine Tech!"

"Uh huh," said Zac.

"It looks like they're behind the *Sea Devil*."

"The *Sea Devil*?" asked Zac.

"The secret deep-sea submarine!" said Leon, sounding impatient. "Marine Tech is going to use it to get to GIB's Safe Talker, hidden on the floor of the West Sea!"

Leon went on. "We thought the Safe Talker was secure because it's 1,200 metres down. But now that Marine Tech has invented the *Sea Devil*, they can easily bug it. I'm working on deactivating the Safe Talker now, but it's going to take at least 24 hours."

Leon finally paused for air. Zac tried to make sense of what he'd said.

"Leon," Zac said finally. "What's a Safe Talker?"

"Only GIB's most important piece of technology ever!" Leon yelled. "Safe Talkers transmit all our secret communications. They're in code, of course. But if anyone got their hands on a Safe Talker, they could switch off the encryption filter. All our communications would be in ordinary English."

"So they'd understand every word," said Zac.

"Yup," said Leon. "And our secrets are pretty high-tech stuff. The enemy could use them to build aircraft, subs, satellites …whatever! Then they could sell them for heaps of money."

"I've always thought it's strange that a small company like Marine Tech invents the coolest stuff first, every single time," said Zac slowly.

"This must be how! They steal other people's secrets," said Leon.

Zac's mind chewed over the mission. "If Marine Tech's after our Safe Talker, won't their sub testing station be somewhere close to it?"

"I'm sure you're right, Zac," said Leon. "Good spying. The Safe Talker's located at 89 degrees west south-west."

Zac programmed it into his GPS. Automatically, the computer calculated the distance Zac would have to travel to reach the Safe Talker.

"It's ages away. It will take me hours just to get there – let alone stop the *Sea Devil* from diving 1,200 metres down to the Safe Talker," said Zac.

"I know. It's 10:43 a.m. now, which only gives you 23 hours to stop the *Sea Devil* diving. You can't waste a second, Zac."

"I'm on it," said Zac, hanging up the SpyPad.

But however much of a hurry Zac was in, he knew he'd be going nowhere if he didn't figure out how to work the amphibious submersible first. He fished the instruction manual out of the trash.

He'd have to read it after all!

CHAPTER FOUR

Zac looked up from the instruction manual. *The forward momentum and downward lift of the wing allows your Personal Amphibious Submersible to literally fly below the water's surface*, he read.

He checked his watch.

It'd taken him more than two hours to figure out how to pilot the submersible properly. No wonder his eyes were watering.

Just then, Zac's SpyPad beeped again. It wasn't the usual beep though. This beep was much louder. The SpyPad only made this kind of beep when there was a special emergency message being broadcast to everyone in the area, not just GIB spies.

Zac grabbed his SpyPad.

MAYDAY

TO ALL VESSELS IN
THE WEST SEA AREA

A small plane has
crashed into the sea.
Two passengers need rescuing.
If you can assist, go immediately
to the crash zone at
72 degrees north north-east.

MESSAGE FROM
WEST SEA OCEAN RESCUE

RESCUE MODE
>>> ON?

If Zac didn't head for the Safe Talker
straight away, he'd fall seriously behind on
his mission. And he couldn't fail – not on
his first solo mission.

But, then again, wasn't his spying job with GIB really all about helping people? And there were two people whose lives were in danger right now.

The crash site was in the opposite direction from the Safe Talker. But Zac had no choice. He changed the coordinates in his GPS system.

He was going to the crash site.

At top speed, Zac raced off in the amphibious submersible, sticking close to the surface. He needed a good view of what was going on.

Zac pressed the "Up Periscope" button on the dashboard. The periscope poked through the water.

Through it, Zac could see what was happening up above. Straight away, Zac saw the plane wreck in the distance. Both wings were broken in half, and Zac could just make out a man and a woman, hanging on as tight as they could. They were waving desperately for help.

But the worst thing was, the plane wreck had just caught fire!

Zac had to get there and save those people before the fire took hold. If the fuel tank caught fire, the plane would explode.

The amphibious submersible flew through the water. But still it seemed too slow! Was he going to make it in time?

Zac checked the periscope.

He was almost there!

"Help us! Somebody! Help us!" yelled the woman.

Zac steered the submersible upward until it broke through the surface of the water. He opened the hatch on the very top of the submersible and stuck out his head.

"Don't panic!" he called to the couple. "I've got everything under control."

But Zac knew that he didn't really have everything under control.

He couldn't just jump out of the amphibious submersible and swim over to the plane wreck to help the people. For a start, he couldn't possibly carry the man and the woman by himself. And what if the plane's fuel tank did explode? Then he'd be killed too.

Zac scanned the cabin for safety gear. Besides Zac's own life jacket, there was only a weird kind of gun with an enormous loop on the end of the barrel. Beside that was a bottle of liquid labelled "RescueBubble."

Could this be what he thought it was? There was only one way to find out!

"Jump!" he yelled to the passengers.

The woman jumped into the water.

But the man was shaking his head. "No, you come here!" the man yelled desperately. "I can't swim!"

"I can't come any closer! You'll have to jump!" cried Zac.

Behind the man, the angry orange flames roared. They licked their way up both wings, higher and higher! They'd be at the fuel tank any second now.

"Now!" yelled Zac.

The man screwed up his face. With a terrified yell, he jumped into the sea.

Zac snatched up the gun and the bottle of RescueBubble.

Zac hoped that the RescueBubble worked a bit like the bubble blowers he'd had as a kid. He poured the RescueBubble liquid into a hole on the top

of the gun and aimed it at the people. He squeezed the trigger.

Just as he thought! A great big bubble formed. It shot toward the couple, who were thrashing about in the sea. The man looked like he was about to drown. The bubble drifted down and swallowed up the people. Instantly, the bubble hardened.

KERRR-**BANG!**

A fireball shot hundreds of metres into the air. The plane exploded!

But inside their giant rescue bubble, both the passengers were safe.

The force of the explosion sent the bubble flying toward Zac, who was hanging out of the hatch on top of the amphibious submersible. Expertly, he caught the bubble.

Zac switched his SpyPad to laser mode and a bright red beam shot out. With one swift movement, Zac sliced the bubble open and freed the people inside. With all his strength, he dragged the man and woman through the hatch and into the amphibious submersible.

"You saved our lives!" said the man, panting. "And we don't even know who you are."

"I'm Power. Zac Power," said Zac, putting out his hand.

CHAPTER... ...FIVE

"Angela Blythe-Jones," said the woman. "And this is my husband, Charles."

"We were flying from our country estate to our beach estate," said Angela.

"And doing some squid-spotting on the way," said Charles. "It's a little hobby of ours. There are quite a few giant squid in the area, you see."

Angela looked at the wrecked, burning

plane. "Next time we go squid-spotting, we'll charter a Learjet," she said.

In all his time as a spy, Zac had never met anyone like the Blythe-Joneses. They must be millionaires.

Or maybe even billionaires!

"How can we repay you for saving us?" asked Angela, her huge diamond ring catching the light as she smoothed her shiny blond hair.

"You don't need to repay me," said Zac.

All the same, he wondered what kind of awesome present the Blythe-Joneses might give him.

A dune buggy? A trip into outer space? A personal robot?

Zac was too busy thinking to notice Charles taking something out of his pocket and writing on it.

"At least let us take a photograph of us all together," said Charles. He took his top-of-the-range digital camera from its waterproof case.

Zac posed as the Blythe-Joneses stood around him. Charles slipped something into Zac's pocket as they smiled for the camera. Zac didn't notice.

Then Zac got his SpyPad out and switched it to Digital Camera mode.

"Take one on mine?" he said, handing the SpyPad to Charles.

Charles snapped away. "I should send

these in to the newspaper," he said. "You'll be a hero, Zac."

A hero!

The words rang in Zac's ears. He'd always hoped that one day he'd be famous for his spying exploits. But he couldn't allow his photograph to be published. He'd never be able to go undercover again.

"Thanks, Mr. Blythe-Jones, but I can't," Zac said. Really, he wanted to say the opposite.

Zac caught sight of the clock in the dashboard.

The rescue operation had taken hours!

"I should drop you off somewhere. You need to rest," said Zac. *And I need to find the Sea Devil in a hurry*, he thought to himself.

Zac scanned his GPS navigation screen for the nearest populated land. There was an Eden Island nearby. Zac punched in the coordinates.

SPY-SCOPE

LOCATION >>> EDEN ISLAND

Half an hour later, Zac sighted land through the periscope. He headed for shore.

"Come in, Eden Island," said Zac into the radio. "Requesting permission to land."

The radio crackled. "State your business. Over."

How rude! The Eden Island Coast Guard must be very overworked.

"Some passengers of mine need to come ashore," said Zac. "There's been a plane crash. Over."

"I read you," came the response, even less friendly than before. "You are cleared to land, but on the north side of the island only."

"Roger that," said Zac, puzzled.

Why wasn't he allowed to land any-where but on the north side? There was something very suspicious going on. But Eden Island was so close now. He had to drop off the Blythe-Joneses and get on with the mission.

Zac lowered the wheels on the bottom of the amphibious submersible. He turned the hydraulic steering column sharply. The amphibious submersible burst through the surface of the water. The next second, Zac was driving up the beach!

Straight away, a man ran over to them. He was dressed in a parka with a large Eden Island crest on the back.

"Are these the people from the plane

crash?" the man asked Zac, narrowing his eyes and looking the Blythe-Joneses up and down.

Zac nodded.

"This way," snapped the official. "There are showers and hot soup waiting for you," he went on, herding the couple away.

"And you," he said, turning to Zac. "I suggest you be on your way. But don't go near the south side of the island, will you?"

Out of the corner of his eye, Zac noticed the huge, craggy mountain towering over the island.

His spy senses were tingling.

"I swear I won't go anywhere near it," he said.

He waved a casual goodbye to the Blythe-Joneses with his left hand. His right hand was in his pocket, fingers firmly crossed.

CHAPTER SIX

Zac raced back to the amphibious submersible. He had a hunch about Eden Island. Sure, it was most likely that Marine Tech's sub testing station was in very deep water. But that craggy island was so big, it could easily hide an entire submarine.

What if Marine Tech were building their subs on Eden Island, then towing them out to deeper water and testing them there?

Following this hunch would be risky. He was a long way off his mission already, and stopping to check out Eden Island would use up even more time. All the same, Zac was a top spy. And taking risks is what top spies do.

Zac was going to investigate Eden Island!

Back in the amphibious submersible, Zac steered down beneath the water. He set a course for half a kilometre from the spot he'd dropped the Blythe-Joneses.

A hundred metres away from shore, Zac killed his engines. He needed to be as quiet as possible.

Silently, he landed and crept up the south side of the island. He looked around.

It was nearly dark, and no one had seen him. Or, at least he didn't think they had.

Just ahead of him, the mountain rose steeply out of the sand. He tapped his belt. Yes, there was his new electronic grappling hook, called the AutoHook. He leaned back and pressed the "release" button. The AutoHook shot out high above his head.

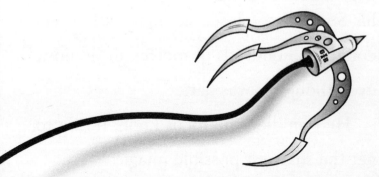

Zac heard a clunk as the grappling hook caught on a rock. He gave the rope a tug. The AutoHook held tight.

He hit the "winch" button. Instantly, he was pulled at top speed through the air toward the hook. When he reached the hook, he held onto the rock as he shot it out high above his head again.

Zac kept doing this all the way to the top of the mountain.

At last, Zac was at the top. He switched his SpyPad to telescopic night-vision. He could see hundreds of metres ahead now, even though it was dark.

He twiddled the focus knob, trying to get the sharpest possible image.

Then he heard it…

CRACK!

A twig snapping!

Zac spun around. Maybe the official had seen him land on the beach, and had followed him up the mountain.

Yes, there was that sound again. But this time, it was followed by the soft pitter-patter of an animal's paws.

Sweat beaded on Zac's forehead. He wiped it away. *It's only a fox.*

Zac turned his attention back to his SpyPad. The image was crisp now. Time to check out what was really hidden on the south side of Eden Island.

It was unbelievable!

Through the SpyPad's powerful telescope, Zac saw people parading up and down the beach. There was no sign of the

Sea Devil. In fact, it looked more like there was a party going on. Everyone was holding cocktails and dancing.

He looked closer.

There was something a bit weird about these people…

Zac's eyes nearly popped out of his head. They weren't wearing any clothes!

Zac's cheeks burned with embarrassment. The south side of Eden Island was a nudist resort! That was why the official didn't want anyone dropping in.

He might have scaled the mountain quickly, but Zac climbed down it even faster.

These people were as old as his mum

and dad. And they were all in the nude! It was just too gross to think about.

In a flash, Zac was back in the amphibious submersible. He sped out to sea. What kind of spy was he when his hunches were so very, very wrong? The clock on the dashboard read 12:34 a.m.

He'd wasted so much time!

CHAPTER... ...SEVEN

Zac settled down in the driver's seat, concentrating hard. No matter how low he felt, he had to get on with the mission. Maybe persistence was really the key to being a top spy.

He re-entered the coordinates for GIB's Safe Talker.

...89°W–SW...

At last, he was on the right track.

All of a sudden —

Whump! Whump! THUD!

The amphibious submersible had hit something, and it was big!

The next moment, the whole sub began rocking up and down violently.

What on earth is happening? wondered Zac.

Zac rushed to the porthole on the right-hand side of the amphibious submersible. He looked out.

Yuck! What are those things?

Through the window, Zac could see thick, black things that were covered with massive round suckers that opened and closed. Zac counted ten in all.

Ten…

Suddenly, Zac had it.

Squids had ten tentacles. The Blythe-Joneses had said there were giant squids in the West Sea. Zac was certain. A giant squid was attacking him!

Up and down, up and down. The amphibious submersible rocked harder than ever!

The squid was so big, it could play with the amphibious submersible like a bath toy. Zac knew he had to free himself, and fast. The submersible might be snapped in half!

He raced to the pilot's seat. He turned the speed dial up as far as it would go. The cockpit lurched as the submersible tried to leap forward. But the squid wouldn't let go.

Angrier than ever, it shook the amphibious submersible again.

Zac flew out of his seat.

The squid had turned the amphibious submersible upside-down! Zac went flying all the way across the cockpit.

Like a bullet, Zac shot toward the hard metal wall.

Crrrrrrr-ACK!

Zac slammed into the wall, head first. The cabin went blurry. He was seeing double! Blood flowed from a cut on his head. He stood up. Then, like a bad guy in a computer game, he slumped to the floor.

Zac was out cold.

CHAPTER... ...EIGHT

Zac opened one eye. There was a deep cut just above it, and a huge, painful lump on his head. He was lying on the ground, stiff and cold. He checked his watch.

How long had he been lying on the ground? He couldn't remember.

He looked around. Nothing around him looked familiar. Where was he?

It looked like he was in some kind of mini-submarine, drifting all by itself somewhere in the middle of the sea. But why would a kid his age be all by himself in a mini-sub?

Zac thought hard for a moment. Who was he? What was his name? He realized he had absolutely no idea.

Zac had totally lost his memory!

It was the weirdest feeling, not even knowing your own name. Frantically, Zac searched the amphibious submersible for clues.

There was a jacket slung over the back

of the pilot's seat. He tried it on. It was his size! It must belong to him.

Zac looked through the pockets. In the left-hand pocket, there was an envelope. Zac tore it open.

It was stuffed with money!

Thousands of dollars.

On the front were the words, "To Zac. You'll always be a son to us. With love and thanks from the Blythe-Joneses."

His name must be Zac!

Zac Blythe-Jones.

It seemed right. Who else would give you an envelope of money except your own parents? And judging by the size of the present, his parents must be very rich.

Perhaps the mini-submarine was some kind of very cool toy.

Just the sort of thing a millionaire's son would have, Zac thought.

Zac searched the other pocket of his jacket. There he found a strange object that looked a bit like a pocket calculator, only with a much larger screen.

"SpyPad," he read on the front.

Some kind of expensive game or digital camera, Zac thought.

He flicked it on.

A photograph popped up. Zac saw himself standing next to a smiling man and woman. His parents!

True, he had brown hair and his mum

and dad were blond. But then again, not all families look alike.

Just then, Zac heard a strange, mournful sound.

PAAAAAAAAAAAAARP!

It was so loud Zac thought his ears might burst. He raced to a porthole to see what had made the sound.

There, right next to him, was the most awesome, high-tech submarine ever.

It was shiny black and bullet-shaped. There was a fancy winged keel underneath. On the front were 20 torpedo launchers. On top, Zac saw two very large surface-to-air missiles.

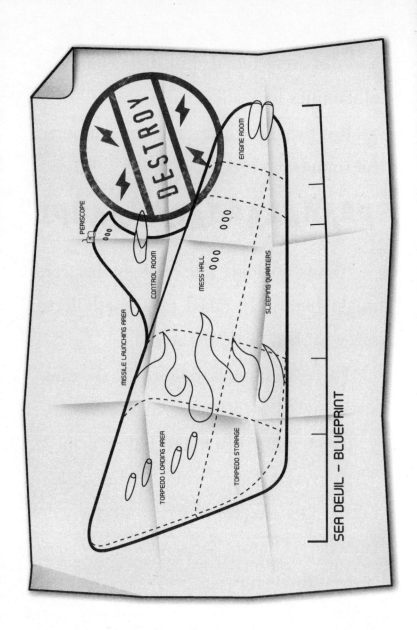

SEA DEVIL – BLUEPRINT

It must be a navy submarine sent especially to rescue him! That must be the kind of thing that happens when your parents are millionaires.

The radio on board crackled to life.

"This is Captain Stewart aboard the *Sea Devil*. Do you read me, over?"

Zac snatched up the radio.

"Yes, I read you! This is Zac Blythe-Jones. I was out for a joyride in my mini-submarine here, but I've injured myself. Can you take me home?"

"You say your name's Zac Blythe-Jones? Over," came the reply.

"Uh huh," said Zac. "I'm a millionaire's son."

There was a pause. Zac started wondering if his radio worked.

"Come aboard then," finally came the voice from the radio. "Steer your submersible toward the rear of the *Sea Devil* and drive into the loading bay."

Even as the voice said this, a large hatch was opening round the back of the impressive black submarine.

Zac leaped into the pilot's seat. He stared at the controls for a second. He wasn't sure exactly how, but somehow he remembered how to work the cool little mini-sub. Maybe he was getting his memory back, even just a little bit.

Zac backed into the *Sea Devil*'s loading

bay easily. The hatch door closed behind him. He was in an airlock. Silently, an interior door slid open. It must lead right into the centre of the *Sea Devil*. He wondered if Captain Stewart could let him have a look around.

Probably, thought Zac. *She seems friendly*.

"Zac Blythe-Jones," boomed a voice over the submarine's PA system. "Proceed immediately to the galley."

The galley? Wasn't that a ship's kitchen?

Excellent. He was just in time for breakfast.

CHAPTER NINE

The galley was full of people in coveralls and diving gear eating breakfast. They all had the same thing written across their backs.

Marine Tech.

Strange. Zac had never heard of it.

A woman in a suit with Marine Tech stitched on the pocket met Zac at the door.

"I'm Captain Stewart," she said, sounding

mean and friendly all at the same time. "How about a bowl of Chocmallow Puffs?"

She showed Zac to a seat.

"So, you're a millionaire's son," said Captain Stewart, casually.

"Yup," said Zac, through mouthfuls of cereal.

"Prove it," said Captain Stewart.

Zac dug in his jacket pocket for the envelope.

"Here, look. My mum and dad gave me all this money. And that was just today!" said Zac.

Captain Stewart's eyes widened. She got up and walked over to a man who was hovering nearby.

"Don't think it's him," she whispered to the man.

"The kid we've got to watch out for is called Power, not Blythe-Jones," said the man. "Should I get HQ to email us a photo of the Power kid, just to make sure?"

"The test dive must go off without a hitch," Captain Stewart said sourly. "Do whatever it takes."

The man nodded and disappeared through a door. Zac caught a glimpse of the office that lay beyond.

Just then, a loud siren went off.

Everyone around him got up and rushed out the door. Zac stood up too. Was he supposed to be going somewhere?

Within seconds, the room was empty except for Zac and Captain Stewart.

"No! Stay where you are, you little… rascal," she finished quickly.

The galley door opened. Someone in a diving suit rushed in.

"Captain Stewart? There's a problem with one of the dive mechanisms. You'd better come."

The woman got up. "Don't you move, Zac," she said, before rushing away.

Zac had a hunch.

Something wasn't right about Captain Stewart. Why didn't she believe he was who he said he was? And who was emailing his photograph?

Maybe these Marine Tech people were trying to kidnap him for his parents' money. He needed to get a look at that email!

But despite being a millionaire's son, Zac was just an ordinary kid. What did he know about following hunches or spying on people?

He took another spoonful of Choc-mallow Puffs, and chewed thoughtfully.

All the same, something buried deep inside was telling him to do something. He was alone now. If there was ever a time to act, this was it.

Zac snuck toward the office door.

It was ajar.

Zac peered through the crack. Inside the office, the man from the galley was sitting behind a computer, his back to the door.

"That's right, Boss. One of the guard-squids picked him up," the man was saying. "Don't think he entered our test zone deliberately. Dumb rich kid just stumbled across it, I think."

As Zac watched, something came up on the computer screen on the man's desk. The man was too busy sucking up to his boss to even notice.

"So, you're sending the photograph now? Just need to be extra doubly certain the kid's not Zac Power," said the man. "Not that he could be, of course," he went on, laughing.

Zac squinted even harder through the crack in the door. He couldn't see what was on the screen. He hooked his finger in the door and slowly, very slowly, opened it wider.

The man coughed.

Zac jumped into the air with fright but the man didn't turn around.

Dropping to all fours, Zac crept into the room. Now he could see the screen perfectly.

On it, he saw a scan of himself.

Underneath he read:

NAME >>> ZAC POWER
OCCUPATION >>> GIB SPY

CHAPTER... TEN

Power? Zac *Power*?

A spy?

In a flash, it came back to him. Marine Tech wanted GIB's Safe Talker! And the only way to stop them was to sabotage the *Sea Devil*'s test dive.

Zac crawled out of the office.

Then, all of a sudden, the floor began to tilt.

A computerized voice said over the PA system, "70 metres."

The dive had just begun! And the computerized voice was counting the depth as the *Sea Devil* descended.

Zac held onto a nearby table leg to stop himself sliding. He needed a plan.

Then, Zac heard a surprised yell coming from the office.

"Ah ha!" came the man's voice. "That kid is Zac Power, after all!"

Oh no! He'd seen the email! Zac was so busy remembering his mission that he hadn't thought to delete it. Zac raced out of the galley just as a siren began wailing.

Captain Stewart's voice boomed over

the loudspeaker. "Attention all personnel! If you see Zac Power, alias Zac Blythe-Jones, capture him. Use whatever force necessary. He is a spy."

Zac tore away down a long, winding corridor, breathing hard. He had no idea which way to go!

"90 metres…120 metres," came the computerized voice over the loudspeaker.

At the end of the corridor, there were two doorways. Which one should he take?

Zac grasped the right hand door. He hesitated. What if he opened this door and found it was full of Marine Tech henchmen? He'd be captured straight away.

He turned to the door on the left.

Again, he stopped. What if this doorway led straight to Captain Stewart?

"150 metres...180 metres," said the loudspeaker.

Zac heard a sound coming up the corridor behind him. Footsteps! And they were getting louder and louder.

He couldn't turn back now. He had to choose one of those doors.

"200 metres."

Zac grabbed the left door handle. He plunged through the door and slammed it shut behind him.

He was in a storeroom. It was filled with rows and rows of torpedoes.

"250 metres...275 metres...300 metres."

Zac had an idea!

He tore off his digital watch. He was no techno geek, but you couldn't get through basic spy training without learning how to make a bomb timer.

"325 metres."

Zac's ears were beginning to pop. The deeper the *Sea Devil* dived, the more his head throbbed with pressure. It hurt, but Zac couldn't stop now.

Hurriedly, he fiddled with the wires from inside his digital watch.

Red over blue.

A twist here. Another there.

That was it! He had it.

Running to the nearest torpedo, Zac

attached the timer. He should have been freaking out, but he wasn't. He had a plan and he was sticking to it, even if it was incredibly dangerous. Zac felt more in control than he had the entire mission.

He set the timer for 60 seconds.

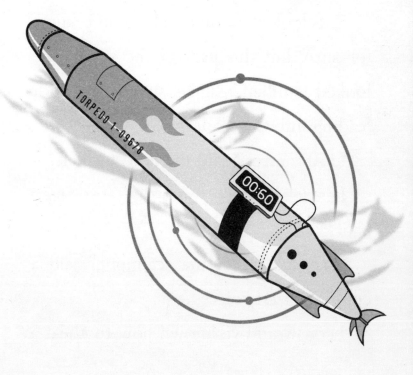

He ran, slamming the storeroom door behind him. He had to get back to his submersible before the *Sea Devil* went much deeper. If things went according to Zac's plan, he was going to destroy the whole storeroom of torpedoes!

Zac looked around. He didn't know for sure, but this part of the submarine looked familiar. Yes! He was at the door leading into the loading bay.

"350 metres," said the loudspeaker.

Beside the door was a digital security panel.

"Prepare for retina scanning," said a computerized voice.

Leon would've known how to cheat a

retina scan and get that door open without force. But Zac didn't have time to call his brother. He took a run up and rammed his shoulder into the door.

It sprang open. And right there, where he'd left it, was his amphibious submersible.

"400 metres…425 metres."

Zac tried the hatch of the amphibious submersible. It was open! He jumped in and slammed the hatch closed.

"450 metres…475 metres."

Fear clutched Zac's stomach. He had a feeling this might happen. His amphibious submersible couldn't go deeper than 450 metres. And the *Sea Devil* was already deeper than that. Would his submersible make it?

But no sooner had Zac thought this than he heard voices at the loading bay door.

"Stop right there, Zac Power!" yelled Captain Stewart.

"525 metres...550 metres."

Captain Stewart practically flew across the loading bay toward the amphibious submersible. She was closing in on him!

"575 metres."

There must be some way Zac could

stop her. He scanned the cockpit for ideas.

His iPod!

Should he? Of all his gadgets, his iPod was his favourite.

But he had no choice!

"600 metres."

Zac opened the hatch. With perfect aim, he threw his iPod through the air like a Frisbee. It smacked Captain Stewart in the head. She dropped to the floor.

Then…

Kerrr-BOOOOOoM!

The storeroom of torpedos exploded. In a shower of white-hot sparks, the thick metal walls of the loading bay ripped open like foil. And a split second later, Zac zoomed through it and away into the open sea.

Zac turned the speed dial up as far as it could go. He shot upward. He couldn't tell how fast — his speedometer had shattered!

The same pressure twisted Zac's brain in his skull. He pinched his nose and breathed out hard. Hopeless! He couldn't clear his ears that way, not at this depth.

His head was going to explode any second! And so was the amphibious submersible!

Great cracks in the glass appeared from nowhere. Water gushed into the cabin. The lights flicked on and off. The submersible veered left. It swung right.

The GPS screen was down!

So was the autopilot.

Zac jammed on manual steering. He had to keep going! But it was like trying to ride a wild bull.

He checked his rear-view mirror. He was drenched. But he was almost at the surface.

There was a loud bang. The amphibious submersible's glass top shattered altogether. Zac took an enormous breath and jumped through the ragged hole.

He'd have to swim the rest of the way!

Zac kicked as hard as he could. His head was spinning. He needed air! He was going to die!

Then…

He burst through the surface.

He gasped. At last! Air!

There was a loud buzzing sound overhead. Zac looked up. Hovering just above him was a Learjet with a rope ladder dangling from it. A tiny figure waved from the doorway.

Zac grabbed the rope ladder. He was exhausted but he hauled himself up it. In a few seconds, he was lying on his back on the floor of the jet, coughing up water.

"Zac?" It was Leon. And he was standing with Charles and Angela Blythe-Jones.

"We were in the area, squid-spotting in this chartered Learjet," said Angela, "when Leon contacted our pilot, wanting to know if we could help with this last tricky stage of the mission."

"Of course, we said yes," smiled Charles.

"I've still got that money you gave me," said Zac. "We're not allowed to keep any money we get on missions."

"Well, how about just a small reward for completing your first solo mission successfully?" said Angela.

She handed him a box. It was a brand new iPod. A top-of-the-line model.

With video.

Leon called Mission Control. He needed to send in a team to tow the *Sea Devil* to shore and arrest everyone on board.

"Hey, Zac?" said Leon, when he'd finished the call. "There are some messages here for you," said Leon. "Big Turtle wants to know if the amphibious submersible's still in one piece."

Zac was silent.

"And Agent Bum Smack…er…I mean, mum…says you've got to come straight home. You've got a test on the life cycle of coral tomorrow."

But Zac wasn't listening. He felt like he was floating. The mangled submersible aside, his first solo mission was a success. And he had a brand new video iPod.

Homework would just have to wait!

...**THE END**...